CW00503103

The Rose Bower

A collection of a dozen
rose-themed short stories

ISBN 978-0-9930222-3-4

Text and cover designed by Shore Books and Design
Blackborough End, Norfolk PE32 1SF

Printed by Biddles Books
King's Lynn, Norfolk PE32 1SF

for my mother with love

Acknowledgements

My thanks to Jemma for her unflagging enthusiam, Grizelda for leading our Creative Writing group, her hospitality and support and to Gloria and Patricia group members for their input and encouragement.

Also to Kelvin I Jones for his illuminating and enjoyable Creative Writing courses.

Finally my thanks to Nigel Mitchell the designer of this book for his professional skills and staunch support.

Some of my Creative Writing course homework assignments developed a rose theme and I thought that they might one day make a collection of short stories.

Contents

The Friend Indeed

Miss Bates was standing at the bus stop, waiting for the number 25. She always caught the number 25. The number 25 would take her from just outside Liverpool Street station deep into the City and she would alight at Holborn. She would walk down a narrow side-street to the courtyard, where her offices, her former offices, for Miss Bates had retired last summer, were situated. The gleaming brass plate by the front door proclaimed, 'Trumpton and Trumpton Solicitors.'

The offices were fronted by a small garden, which consisted of a strip of grass, bordered by flower beds, and edged by low, black-enamelled railings. Miss Bates had developed and tended the garden for all the years of her employment with Trumpton and Trumpton and now, in her retirement, came up to the City especially from her home in the suburbs, which she shared with her elderly mother, on the first Thursday of the month to tend it again.

She carried two doughty, capacious bags.

One held her gardening impedimenta, her trowel, fork, secateurs, black plastic bag for debris and very often plants from her garden at home, carefully wrapped in damp newspaper to replace jaded plants in the office garden. The other contained her handbag, her elevenses, as she didn't like to bother the young secretaries, and her lunch. This was usually an egg and watercress sandwich with a yoghurt to follow. She was a great believer in 'not going to work on an empty stomach' and 'feeding the inner woman,' which might have accounted for her rotund shape. 'Not going to work on an empty stomach,' was a tenet she used to share with Mr William, when she would take him his elevenses of coffee and biscuits, or tea and cake at four o'clock.

The supplies for these ministrations came from the shop on the far corner of the street. A corner shop with an impressive delicatessen selection and the special blends of tea and coffee, of which Mr Patel, the owner, was so proud. There was also a couple of small, wrought iron tables with matching chairs for light refreshments. The shop had been there for as long as she could remember and she had become an old and valued customer.

In due season the office garden would

boast snowdrops, wallflowers, grape hyacinths, followed by daffodils, crocus and tulips. The bright annuals and perennials of summer succeeded them and the garden was a blaze of colour from the early clematis to the splendour of the wisteria, honeysuckle and roses in summer. There followed the rich hues of autumn, dahlias, and chrysanthemums, which gave way to the winter heathers and red-berried shrubs. At Christmas, Miss Bates always brought a holly wreath, bright with red ribbons, which she had made from her holly tree at home to decorate the office front door. Mr William was always so appreciative of this.

Her pride and joy however was the climbing rose, which adorned the front wall. Mr William had suggested this addition to the garden. His wife shared his passion for roses and had chosen 'Gloire de Dijon,' a favourite climbing rose, which they had in abundance at home. Mr William had asked Miss Bates to earmark in the diary a suitable Friday morning for 'gardening fatigues'. He duly arrived, sporting unaccustomed casual wear, check shirt, sweater, corduroy trousers and boots and had brought with him some good soil from home, a bag of well-rotted manure and a stout spade. The specially purchased 'Gloire de

Dijon' had rewarded this excellent beginning and subsequent care and every summer the profusion of perfectly formed, richly fragranced, apricot blooms was a sight to behold.

Mr William had arrived to join the family firm just as she had begun work there and she often reflected that they had learned the ways of Trumpton and Trumpton together. He had retired just before she had. She had attended his funeral only last summer, the little village church packed with mourners. Mr Richard, his son, had invited her back to the house afterwards and she had accepted, despite feeling that she did not belong. The old, mellow brick manor house was set amid beautiful gardens, manicured lawns, and meticulously trimmed shrubs, conveying a sense of timelessness, spaciousness, and peace. And the glory of the roses. She could imagine Mr William spending time here. He would have been so lonely following the death of his wife the previous year.

Mr Richard had asked her to help with the organisation of the Memorial Service for his father, which was to take place in a nearby Wren church in the City. He had particularly asked her to help with the choice of music, for he knew she was acquainted with Mr William's taste, as they had attended, separately, lunchtime concerts in nearby City churches, and discussed them together afterwards. On Mr William's death, she had cut a few roses from the office garden and had made them into a posy for him, as well as contributing generously to the office wreath.

She kept a small watering can under the sink in the office kitchen, a lightweight pair of shears with which she cut the strip of grass and a small piece of old carpet for a kneeler. She wished in many ways that the garden could have been bigger but she introduced such colour, shape and structure as she could and added to the planting space by the use of terracotta pots, which burgeoned according to season. The front door was flanked by two small bay trees in pots, which Miss Bates had trimmed to pleasing and matching shapes.

Often, as she worked in the garden, she would inspire herself to renewed effort by the promise that she would call in at the corner shop on her homeward way to the bus stop. She would treat herself to something nice for supper, perhaps a slice of pie or quiche, and some olives, or merely be guided by Mr Patel's good taste. He would first of course make solicitous enquiries about her mother's health and she would reciprocate and ask after Mr Patel's aged mother.

Today however was different. When she arrived, Mr Richard stood in the black-lacquered doorway as she approached. There was an air about him that presaged something important.

'Come in Miss Bates, come in to father's office and sit down,' he said, as he ushered her in. The office had been preserved as it always had been. Mr Richard's own office was a much more modern affair, but this room was reserved for clients of his father's age and taste. It was furnished with a huge mahogany desk, behind which was a large leather chair, and an old-fashioned standard lamp, all legacies from Mr William's father before him.

Mr William's black umbrella was still suspended from the old-fashioned antler hat stand. She wondered if the bottom drawer of the desk still contained the souvenir fragments of the bomb, hoarded by Mr William's father, which had fallen on the building in the war. It had been impossible to open that drawer, even though it was not locked, so heavy were the pieces. Miss Bates negotiated the expanse of deep carpet and settled herself in the chair opposite Mr Richard, who began to speak, while she observed that he might be his father's son, but he wasn't nearly as tall, handsome or charming.

'The time had come. Changes. Economic situation. The future. Move to new chambers with his brother-in-law. Their senior partner retiring. Made sense. Regrets. Three months. End of the lease. Questionable future for the garden. Appreciation of all her years of devoted service. Token of their esteem.'

Miss Bates only heard key fragments of Mr Richard's speech, crashing in her head like falling slates, as she was told of the plans for the future. Then Mr Richard was handing her a beautifully-wrapped box. She rose to accept it, thanked Mr Richard, wished him well, picked up her bags, collected her shears and watering-can and waddled out. Her rose was in full bloom. Miss Bates extracted the secateurs from her bag and clipped a small bunch, which she carefully placed on top of her bag, for remembrance, a souvenir. She said her tearful farewell, as she looked lovingly at the garden for the last time and made straight for the corner shop like a homing pigeon.

Mr Patel greeted her warmly. He had known her for many years, as she often in the old days, popped in for special refreshments for meetings with important clients. Mr Patel had even stocked Mr William's favourite cigars. He knew the value of customer service and satisfaction.

'Miss Bates, are you quite well dear lady?' he asked, as her tears fell.

'It's the changes you see Mr Patel, it comes as a shock at my time of life. My little garden. The building is to be sold and my little garden, who can say what will become of my little garden? And my beautiful rose.'

'I can see that it is most distressing for you dear lady.'

'Oh it is!' she exclaimed, groping for her hanky and dabbing at her eyes.

'Come dear lady, you must not upset yourself. Here, come and sit at my table. Some tea. Let me make you a pot of my excellent high-quality tea. It is a new blend and highly recommended.'

'No, really Mr Patel, I couldn't possibly,' said Miss Bates, as she nevertheless plonked her self down gratefully at the table, her impedimenta splaying round her feet.

'I couldn't possibly give you the trouble.'

'It is no trouble at all, dear lady, just some water for your beautiful roses and the boiling of the kettle,' he soothed, taking her plump little hand and patting it gently.

A Time to Reap

The shed was his, his own space, his own unassailable territory. The gardens didn't really belong to him, and of course neither did the grand old house, but the shed, that was a different matter.

In fact the house, the gardens, the cottage and his shed, all belonged to the Bloomsbury family. He had served the family since his apprenticeship, all those years ago, as had his father and grandfather before him. His large, old shed was immaculate. It had a sweet smell, with a trace of fresh soil in the air. Hessian sacks basked in the sunlight under the windows and bunches of herbs were hanging up to dry. Small tools and garden impedimenta were housed in serried racks, with larger tools neatly stored down one end. Flowerpots, washed and dried before storage were stacked according to size. Bales of netting, assorted canes, wooden seed trays, raffia, twine and secateurs were kept at one end of the long, old wooden bench he used for many tasks including potting on. His favourite pruning knife, honed to sharpness, the handle worn to a patina from years of use lay in pride of place.

The house was quite a grand affair, built in the 18th century and the grounds were landscaped with groups of trees, now in gnarled symmetry, the spaces between offering views of the lake. The kitchen garden, which still supplied good, fresh produce for the somewhat depleted household was enclosed by walls, which supported espaliered fruit trees, and the outer walls were covered in climbing roses.

The water garden had been developed at a later date with several pools of various size, the larger with central fountains emanating from sculptures. The largest of these depicted a dolphin, bearing a boy on its back, both playing together for eternity among the sparkling streams of water. The edges of the pools were fringed with iris and an array of water-loving plants and there were small decorative shrubs along the paths, which linked the pools, at their best when studded with water-lilies in bloom.

The rose garden was laid out with walks with decorative iron arches, which supported climbing roses, trained along the connecting ironwork. The arches were also covered in due season by early spring and summer clematis, and the later flowering varieties together with honeysuckle. Wooden seats, which offered the facility to sit and savour the sights and fragrances of the garden, were provided at intervals along the clipped box and billowing, lavender-bordered rose walks. An underground tunnel linked the rose garden with the water garden, specially built in his grandfather's day to shelter the gardeners, while they walked between the gardens. The entrance was a mellow, brick structure with roses growing round it.

He had begun his apprenticeship under his father's tutelage in the kitchen garden. There were several other gardeners then and an older man, officially retired, for odd jobs and the maintenance of the greenhouses. As a lad, he had enjoyed digging and manuring the soil, planting seeds directly in the finely raked tilth, and in due season the satisfaction of preparing vegetables for the house. Every morning he would dig up the vegetables, scrape off the soil, trim and wash them in buckets under the tap, dry them off and arrange them in baskets to take to the kitchen. They first had to pass the scrutiny of his father, and then Cook, who would cast a discerning eye over them, give him a freshly baked treat from the oven for his trouble and send her compliments to his father. He would take the opportunity to exchange a shy glance with the little kitchen maid, Kitty.

He also liked to gather flowers for the house, learning how to choose which blooms to cut and how to prepare them. Every morning he would take the long trugs to the kitchen, and when in season, a perfect rose just breaking bud for her Ladyship's breakfast tray, with a special flower for her husband's buttonhole.

Lady Bloomsbury was particularly fond of the roses but took a keen interest in all the gardens and engaged in long conversations with his father, just as her mother had done before her with his grandfather. She would walk through the rose garden after breakfast and at various times during the day, escorting visitors to the house and sometimes sitting in the shady arbour to read or enjoy the surroundings in contemplative thought. Then in the evening she would always return to walk again through the rose garden to savour the rich fragrances and 'to say goodnight to her roses.'

He was particularly proud of the rose he had developed himself, pollinating with delicate paint brushes, and nurturing it on. After some perseverance he got his rose. Over time it became strong and flourished in established maturity. It was one of Lady Bloomsbury's favourites and he asked if he could name it after her, and she consented with delight. It was a beautiful specimen. A quartered rose of deep, purplish red, strong and vigorous with a glorious fragrance. It was a climber and held pride of place on the outer kitchen wall, from where he had intended to transplant it to a more prestigious setting in the rose walk. But Lady Bloomsbury insisted it stayed where it was. She didn't want it uprooted. She did not favour change for the sake of it.

He had recalled that conversation all those years ago, after Lady Bloomsbury's daughter had come that morning to tell him of her proposed changes, the general improvements and the redevelopment of the stable block. The kitchen garden, his lovingly espaliered fruit cordons on the kitchen wall with their climbing roses on the outside and the rose garden itself would all have to go. They would be keeping on his assistant, the under gardener of course for the time being and the boy. She was very sorry and of course he could stay on in the cottage for the duration of his lifetime in accordance with her mother's Will and . . . .

But he had stopped listening. He had heard enough. When she had gone at last, harsh, clicking high heels fading away on the flags outside, he sat still, immersed in thought. He sat motionless at his bench for a long time, oblivious of time passing.

Then he looked round the shed at nets of onions drying in the rafters, at the bookshelves with his father's and grandfather's old gardening books, his father's gardening boots, his old army boots, still tidily stored beneath. He glanced at the stack of ledgers, where they had faithfully recorded the dates of the plantings and their results over all the years, with their handwritten notes in the margin.

He ran his fingers over his grandfather's pipe-rack, complete with pipes, and the waft of strong tobacco smoke came back to him with snatches of remembered conversations with his grandfather and his father and their wisdom, boundless knowledge and respect for old gardening lore. He studied the collection of framed sepia photographs of distinguished visitors to the garden with the family. His gaze lingered on the photograph of the young Lady Bloomsbury, long before her marriage, with her elder brother, who had been killed in a riding accident. It was through his untimely death that in due course, following the death of her mother, Lady Bloomsbury had inherited the estate.

He glanced at the old basket chair, with its faded cushions, a gift from her Ladyship for his father, so that he could sit in comfort and enjoy the garden at his leisure. He remembered his father's strong, soil-engrained fingers, as gentle as a mother with a baby, tending his seedlings. He thought of Kitty, so young and pretty and even more shy than he had been. But she only had eyes for the footman, and in due course he had got another position and she had gone with him as his wife. So many memories, all entwined with memories of Lady Bloomsbury when young and later with her husband, always interested in the gardens, always appreciative. And then the new regime and now even more changes.

He realized that the time had come. Everything in due season. 'A time to sow and a time to reap' that's what his grandfather used to say. In any case he knew with sad conviction that his time had come. He laid his weather-beaten hand on the bench and with the skill and precision with which he performed every task, took up his pruning knife and cut deep into the vein, a clean, precise, pruning cut.

They said he had 'green fingers,' but the sap that welled forth was a deep, purplish red, the colour of his favourite rose, his own creation, 'The Lady Bloomsbury.'

The Rescue

'Madame Alfred Carriere' was flamboyant, reckless, devil-may-care, some said no better than she ought to be, rampant even. She was also, reliable, tenacious and perfect in form and fragrance. She had breeding and background, but she was most assuredly out of control, or so thought Mr Wicks. Mr Wicks did not approve of 'Madame Alfred', not one little bit. He dismissed her as blowzy, and a climber in the worst possible sense.

'That rose'll have to go. It's out of control, I'm going to tackle it this afternoon.'

'Yes dear,' said Mrs Wicks.

But despite her apparent acquiescence, Mrs Wicks knew that she couldn't let this happen. Mrs Wicks had a deep affection for 'Madame Alfred' and had known, and indeed loved her, for many a summer and was her staunch ally. She decided that some intervention was necessary. Planning, strategy, tactics were called for.

She considered what she might do. She could of course change the menu for lunch.

Something heavier than the quiche, potato and green salads she had planned. Something much more stolid, of a more slowing down nature was called for. Something to lay heavy on the stomach and necessitate some time to digest. A serious snooze would be required, with the newspaper, in the deep comfort of a favourite, imprisoning armchair. Her steak and kidney pudding would fit the bill. Steak and kidney it would be then.

Familiar, appetising, comforting aromas issued from the kitchen and when lunch time came, Mr Wicks was very happy to sit down, tuck in and hoover up every morsel of his favourite dish and then subside into his armchair. There was no possibility of stirring for some time, let alone lugging the ladder out of the shed with a view to undertaking any pruning. Mrs Wicks, having washed up and set the kitchen to rights, made her way to where 'Madame Alfred' was besporting herself in the warmth of the afternoon. Mrs Wicks settled herself in her garden chair, took up her needles and began to knit contentedly and companionably in the company of her old friend.

However, her husband persisted in the

notion that 'Madame Alfred' had outstayed her welcome and Mrs Wicks grew more anxious. She had managed to keep Mr Wicks so actively engaged with jobs of varying size and urgency, that the summer had passed in a busy whirl of occupation for him, so much so that he had not had time or energy to return to the subject.

But when the summer days grew somewhat shorter and even before they began to give way to the first mellow mists of autumn, he began to consider cutting back, a general pruning. To be fair, he started with the hedges and when they were subdued it was the turn of the shrubs and the perennials and then 'that rose'.

Mrs Wicks found several excuses to interrupt him and his work did not progress quite as smoothly as Mr Wicks would have wished. Then the issue, for issue it was by now, of 'Madame Alfred' was raised.

'I don't know what you're making such a fuss about. It's only a rose.'

'Yes dear,' said Mrs Wicks.

Though his words scalded her heart, Mrs Wicks as usual gave no sign, as she reflected that it was she, in the first place, who had introduced 'Madame Alfred', when they came to live there. To think of that north-facing wall now, without her stunning presence, her clusters of double white flowers, flushed with a soft pink, and her beautiful fragrance would be impossible.

'I am going to prune it, give it a bit of a tidy up.'

'Yes dear,' said Mrs Wicks.

But Mrs Wicks knew of what excesses he was capable with a pruning knife in his hand. She went off to the shed soon afterwards with the intention of hiding the pruning knives. She caught sight of the pruning saw, hanging up along with the other saws and the ladder. It occurred to her that she might saw through part of a rung. He would of course fall and thereby cool his ardour. She banished this foolish fantasy immediately. However, while she sat knitting in the late summer sunshine that afternoon, she guiltily shared her fantasy with 'Madame Alfred', who fluttered her leaves, nodded her blooms and wafted her sweet fragrance in response.

Then the day dawned. Mr Wicks assembled the ladder, the pruning saw, and the wheelbarrow and began his assault.

Mrs Wicks heard the yell from the sanctuary of her kitchen and hurried out. Mr Wicks was several feet up, the ladder had fallen away and he was clinging on to her branches as 'Madame Alfred' clung, with the help of her wires, to her wall. Mrs Wicks momentarily wished she had a camera to hand. She stifled the thought, and righted the ladder with difficulty. Mr Wicks carefully lowered himself on to it and descended safely to terra firma. He looked shaken.

'Cup of tea dear, good for shock,' said Mrs Wicks firmly, as she guided him towards the kitchen.

She pushed him gently into his chair, made him a cup of tea, gave him two of his favourite biscuits and then left him to his own devices. She went to see what had befallen her old friend. She found only a few clippings in the wheelbarrow, nothing to speak of. Mr Wicks had slipped before he had had a chance to get going in earnest.

'You saved him,' she said, 'Merci, ma chere Madame.' And 'Madame Alfred' rustled her leaves, nodded her fading blooms and wafted her more muted fragrance by way of reply.

Mrs Wicks returned to the house.

'Better dear?'

'I don't know what happened. One minute I was steady as a rock and the next I was clinging on for dear life.'

'Yes dear,' said Mrs Wicks, 'I think 'Madame Alfred' did you a good turn. She saved you.'

Half-way through his second cup of tea Mrs Wicks added, 'better not disturb her, she's earned her place there now.'

'S'pose she has, s'pose she has at that old girl,' said Mr Wicks philosophically, helping himself to another biscuit.

Siren Song

There was no money. No money at all and that was most certainly that. His hopes of Art College were not going to materialise. He knew that on his next birthday, he would have to forego any hope of Art College, leave school and go in search of work.

His widowed mother somehow kept the family, which consisted of himself and his younger brother, together. But now he was to seek his place in the world. It was not long after the war and austerity was abundant. His mother worked up at the Hall, helping with the cooking, cleaning and sewing and the cottage they lived in was rented from the local farmer, Mr Wakefield. Mr Wakefield's brother had set up in business on his own. He had sold his share of the inherited farm to his brother and started a small garden nursery business. His interest was in growing vegetables, plants, and roses, not growing crops.

On this bright, summer morning, Mrs Dignan urged her son to hurry and gave him a final inspection before they walked the length of Long Lane together to the Nursery. She had already had a word with Mr Wakefield and he had invited her to bring the lad along, promising to 'see what we can do'. And so it was. The lad was not strong, a bit on the weedy side but the fresh air and hard work would sort him out. He was from a good home, and Mr Wakefield had had a lot of time for his father, who had been lost at Dunkirk.

'Well son,' boomed Mr Wakefield, 'we can but give you a chance. You want to do this,' he asked, waving a strong arm in the general direction of the land outside.

'Yes sir.'

'And what do you know about it?'

'I can learn sir.'

'Mm,' said Mr Wakefield. 'I dare say you can and there's a lot to learn. Especially about the roses and it's always hard work on the land.'

He gave them a short tour of the site, telling them the fair but modest starting wage, and what the hours were en route.

He added gruffly, 'you'd better take pot luck with me for your dinner,' certain that the hot soup and pasty, or bread and cold meat, or cheese and pickles that he enjoyed at dinnertime would do the lad some good.

He remembered only too well what fresh air and hard work did to a young appetite, and it would of course take some of the strain off the family budget. He omitted to say that his wife would ply them with mugs of steaming tea throughout the day and slices of her home-made cake. Mr Wakefield also omitted to say that the lad would be welcome to borrow his old bike till he had arranged the weekly payments to the local shop for the purchase of a bike of his own. All in good time.

'Well then,' Mr Wakefield continued, 'would Monday do to start?' and mother and son beamed their delighted thanks and said that indeed it would.

* * *

Another hugely successful Chelsea Flower Show, and the accolade of gold medals for their new roses introduced this year. The internationally acclaimed rose breeder surveyed the stand in all its magnificence and resisted the urge to tweak a bud. His eldest son had masterminded the display as he had for some years now and he knew better than to tweak.

The young journalist was saying 'Dignan's Roses have won yet more medals this year at Chelsea and one of the new roses is called 'Journey's End.' Does that mean you might be retiring? All ambitions achieved with even more accolades and homage from the world-wide industry itself.'

'Retiring?' he hadn't really thought about that. His sons had more or less taken over the day to day running of the business but he had control, his hand was always firmly on the tiller.

'How did it all begin?' the young journalist asked eagerly, forgetting the cool persona to which she aspired. She worked for the local paper in the small town near to his Nursery and had a genuine interest in the celebrated rosarian and his work.

And suddenly the years fell away and he was walking the length of Long Lane with his mother on that bright, summer morning. He told her his story in brief, the beginnings at Wakefields, the need to branch out on his own, the early struggles.

She listened intently, spellbound by his story, and the passion that permeated it.

'Do you think if you hadn't found the roses as you did, if your mother had gone in the other direction to find work for you, would the roses have found you? Is it a calling? Destiny?'

She blushed at the earnestness of the question. It was not lost on him, his eye for detail, his eye for beauty. He noted the pink flush over the golden tinged, perfectly sculpted cheek and the patina of downy golden hairs upon it, peach like, delectable.

A man of few words, he didn't reply. Instead he deftly plucked two roses from the display, handed one to her and fixed the other in his buttonhole, replacing the previous incumbent.

'Smell that!' he said, a command more than an invitation. She closed her eyes, the better to concentrate on breathing in the intoxicating scent and opened them to savour the pure perfection of the flower. A drift of perfectly sculpted, pale pink petals, tinged with gold and a deeper pink flush at the throat, peach like, delectable.

'Breathtaking!' she pronounced.

'Another new rose for my 30th anniversary year at Chelsea. Perhaps that might answer your question. I've called it 'Siren Song.'

The Parting Gift

She was back at the large, forbidding, old Victorian house on the hill called Brentwood Hall, an institution which instilled fear in all who saw it. Originally a workhouse, in its latest incarnation it was a Mental Hospital. As a former patient, she recalled the loathsome electrical therapy and wondered if it had been entirely good for her and her poor, depressed spirit.

But Brentwood Hall had had a face-lift, and this time it was far less daunting, with Redstone Ward redecorated in pastel colours. The long refectory tables were laid for tea with bright gingham table-cloths and interspersed at intervals, small jars of freshly-picked flowers from the gardens. Her own small room had brightly-coloured new curtains and a board on the wall on which to pin reminders, cards, photographs etc. It was all so much more attractive and welcoming than she remembered.

This time there was to be no more electrical therapy for her, just a period of supervised medication and rest. As the weeks passed by, she became well enough to take more notice of her fellow patients. She observed that those, who had been in residence for longest and were due to be discharged, were busy with small duties, filling the water jugs, laying the tables with cutlery, paper napkins and tumblers. She watched them going about their tasks and envied them their purpose and application.

As the days wore on there were sessions of talking to a nurse or therapist and group therapy sessions. There were also periods of inactivity, spent alone in her room staring out at the gardens. She missed her own home and garden. It was all too much for her now, but she continued to struggle on with it, not able to face up to the alternatives. Her son lived nearby and came to cut the grass, not once a week as she would have liked, but just when he could manage it. The hedges needed cutting back and the front fence had been vandalised again and needed repair. And the weeds were out of control. She worried about the upkeep and maintenance of both the house and the garden, only too aware that she couldn't manage as she used to, but fearful of the prospect of change and upheaval.

She spoke mainly with Sister Josephine,

who had been there for some years and whom she remembered from previous visits. Sister Josephine would sometimes ask her about her life and she found it easy to talk to her and to tell her about her life as a young girl, then as a married woman and the mother of a son. She spoke too of her husband's lengthy illness and death and her subsequent widowhood. She even told Sister Josephine about her childhood and the first birthday present that she could remember from some sixty-five years ago, when she was four years old.

Mrs Mead, her grandmother's neighbour had given her a small basket, lined with pretty, cotton fabric. It contained small jars of Mrs Mead's home-made jams and honey from her own bees. In one corner there was a small bunch of salad vegetables, lettuce, radish, and spring onions from the garden tied with raffia. Two small eggs from her own bantams nestled in hay in another. In the other corners were small cork-stoppered, former medicine bottles, now filled with her own rose-hip syrup and blackcurrant cordial. Best of all, on the top there was a small posy of rose-buds, from white and palest pink to deepest red. She remembered her delight at this gift, walking along the garden path to the old greengage tree, carrying the basket just for the sheer pride of ownership and the anticipation of the pleasures to come.

As the weeks passed by she seemed to be getting better, less depressed, and was promoted to undertake the duties of clearing away the plates after meals and stacking them on the trolley and laying the tables for the next meal. She soon found where everything was kept and enjoyed the sense of being useful.

She had also made a friend in Neil, a kindly kindred spirit, whom she found she could talk to easily. He had had his own business, but it had all become too much for him after his divorce and his only son's ongoing drink problem. He was going home next week. He had given her his telephone number and invited her to ring him when she was due to leave with a view to meeting up one day for afternoon tea in her local tea-shop. He lived in the next town and could drive over. She wasn't sure about that as she didn't usually care to socialise, but nevertheless kept his card in her apron pocket, (she liked to wear an apron in the day as she did at home) and would finger it from time to time, like a sort of talisman.

Her son visited her a couple of times a week

and it was good to see him but she began to realise there wasn't much to say. However, some people had no visitors at at all and she must be grateful, for to be so lonely would be very difficult to bear.

The weeks wore on and she could see the hospital gardens burgeoning outside. Her room overlooked a border with large shrubs and perennials. She noticed the huge, colourful lupins in particular and the roses. There was a climbing rose, which looked like a wild rose and the border was studded with shrub roses of every hue. She thought about her garden at home and knew that her first task would be to do some cutting back in order to assess the situation and see what was what. Not so much 'the Chelsea chop' as 'the Brentwood bash' she mused.

Then the eagerly anticipated day of her discharge dawned, and it was also her birthday. There was a special birthday tea with an iced cake and candles. Everyone made a fuss of her with a card that they had all signed and a beribboned bouquet of flowers. Her son was there ready to drive her home.

Sister Josephine approached her with a small gift of her own. She unwrapped it then and there to reveal a small basket of goodies, just like the one she had described from her childhood. But best of all there was a small posy of rose-buds on the top, carrying the same, unchanging, time-honoured message over all the years.

In Memoriam

Jenny was visiting Belthorpe House, courtesy of her local art appreciation group. She had glimpsed the intriguing sculpture earlier on, through a gap at the beginning of a secluded rose-walk, but the guide had swept the group on past it. Now they had come round to the other side of the lake and she saw it again and wanted to take a closer look at it. She manoeuvred her way to the back of the group, listening still to the guide's commentary. When he indicated that they should all move on again and to the left, she side-stepped to the right and broke free of of the group.

The sculpture was in the middle of a narrow rose-walk which led down to the lake. It portrayed a young woman, wearing draped Grecian style robes and holding a rose. Her head was inclined towards it with a graceful arch of her neck. The sculpture was finely wrought and there was a delicacy about the young woman's face as she bent to look at the rose that was haunting and poignant.

Jenny was curious about the origin

of the sculpture as it bore just a simple commemorative plate with an inscription and the dates of the young woman's birth and death and there was, as she discovered, no mention of it in the guidebook. In another section about the family, there was a note to the effect that the youngest daughter of the family in that period had died when young. Jenny wondered what the sad young woman's story had been, and what sort of life she had led. She sat down close by, looked up at the statue and squinted at the sunlight. She took out her picnic lunch and continued to think about the sad young girl. She finished her picnic, the sun grew hotter, the sculpture shimmered in the heat and the scent of the nearby roses became almost overpowering.

* * *

Louise pranced down the rose walk to the lake and cavorted around it. She was so happy that she was going to see Henry today. He had been away in London for a few weeks but he had sent a note requesting to meet her and she could hardly wait for the appointed hour. Would today be the day he would propose?

Had he already spoken with her father and asked for his permission to marry her? But why had Mama not mentioned it to her? Of course she would accept. But should she pretend to consider his proposal and make him wait a little for her reply? She rehearsed her acceptance and experimented with a few demure poses and then abandoned herself to her youth, love of life, and the perfection of the summer's day. She cavorted round the lake, laughing aloud, as she thought that as a sedate married lady her cavorting days would soon be over.

* * *

Jenny continued to gaze at the statue and to think about the young girl. The plaque simply said, 'Louise May Florence, beloved daughter, forever in our thoughts' and gave the dates of her birth and death. So she was only 18 years old when she had died. Only 18 and today was the anniversary of her death. What had happened to her? There was no further information to be had from the guidebook. How frustrating Jenny thought as she gazed up at the sculpture before gradually succumbing to the heat and dozing off.

* * *

Three o' clock on the appointed day of Mr Henry's visit and Milly, Louise's maid had put the finishing touches to her young mistress' hair and they had both giggled with delight. They were the same age and Louise's mother knew she had to keep a close eye on them. They were great friends and there was some giggling but her Mother felt it was nothing that couldn't be managed with care. She thought back to her own youth and her own little maid, who had since become her trusted housekeeper and valued confidante.

Louise walked down the stairs, through the house and out to the rose-walk where she would receive Henry. But when he approached, Louise's heart almost stopped beating for Henry looked so handsome, so purposeful and so very solemn. His face wore a grave expression and it was almost as if he had bad news to impart.

He suggested they walked down to the lake. On the way, he said he had a difficult thing to tell her. The fact was, that although he would always treasure their friendship, his feelings for her were not those of a future husband. He had met someone in London some time ago and in fact their engagement would be announced at the end of the month. Of course he wanted her to know in advance of that and he was sorry if he she had ever believed there could have been a different outcome for them. He took his leave of her and left her in the rose-walk. She watched till he was out of sight, the tears coursing down her cheeks blurring her vision. She buried her face in the roses and sobbed out her despair and what she believed to be the ruin of her young life.

After a little while, it was Milly that Louise's mother sent to find her. Milly picked up her long black skirts with one hand, held her white lace cap to her head with the other and scurried through the gardens to the rose-walk as fast as her high-buttoned boots would let her. She found her young mistress in floods of tears and hugged her close. Louise blurted out the purport of Henry's statement.

Milly gasped and then said, 'oh my lor' Miss, 'e never said that 'ow could 'e Miss.'

Then collecting herself, Milly remembered

to tell her young mistress that her mother wanted to see her in the morning room. They returned slowly to the house together, but not until Milly had plucked a pure, white rose and handed it to her mistress saying, 'ere you are Miss, you 'ave this, it'll make you feel better.' Louise took to her bed and became progressively weaker.

The doctor said the condition would take its course but she had no interest in anything, ate very little and preferred to stay mostly in her room throughout the remainder of the long days of the summer. Then in the autumn she developed an infection, which she didn't have the strength to withstand and succumbing to it seemed to have no desire to regain her health. Her condition steadily declined, and following the celebration of Mr Henry's marriage the next summer she breathed her last.

Her parents in due course commissioned a sculpture as a memorial. Milly, who had no family, was allowed to continue in employment at the house and became lady's maid to Louise's mother, when the time came some years later for her own maid to retire. Every day Milly would steal away to the statue by the lake and pluck a pure, white rose and place it at its foot. Louise's mother would also visit the memorial always alone, her husband having taken to spending most of the day confined to his study with whisky his constant companion. She would notice the freshly-picked rose at its base and know that it was poor, grieving little Milly who had faithfully placed it there.

* * *

Jenny woke up, the sun had gone in and there was a cool breeze blowing. She shivered as she heard the guide calling to her. They were about to tour the house and he had come to collect her. She approached the sculpture one last time and saw something fluttering at its base, which hadn't been there before. She looked more closely and saw that it was a freshly-picked, pure white rose.

The Mother of the Bridegroom

It was the day of the wedding and the mother of the bridegroom took a long, last look at herself in the full-length mirror and decided that 'she'd do'. Actually, she was rather pleased with the soft dove-grey ensemble. She was particularly pleased with the flattering half-veil adorning the elegant hat, whose frondy feathers waited to be stirred by any passing breeze. Yes, she'd definitely 'do,' and so she proceeded to glide gracefully down the stairs.

Her son strode purposefully towards her, tall and heartbreakingly handsome in his 'new for the wedding,' suit and handed her a beautifully-crafted buttonhole. A perfect, fat pink rose-bud, nestling in a delicate arrangement of leaves and fern. Dew was still upon it and the scent was magical.

'Here you are Mum, this is a special one for you, the er mother of the bridegroom,' he said awkwardly.

He planted a kiss on her cheek and rushed off to resume his 'about to be married duties' with his best man. A tear sploshed down on to the rose-bud and she carefully wiped it away. She sat down for a moment and the memory of another buttonhole from years ago, from her childhood, when she was just four years old, flashed into her mind.

The old-fashioned country bus had drawn up at the bus stop and its passengers had begun to alight. And there was Mr Sullivan in a bulky, brown tweed suit clambering down the steps. He lumbered towards her, fiddled with his lapel and handed her his buttonhole, a fat pink rose-bud. It epitomised the summer's day and her childhood, set against the backdrop of fields of buttercups, dotted with black and white Friesian calves. She smiled at the memory. Mr Sullivan, his huge sow called Sarah and his roses.

She was always taken to see Sarah, when she had given birth to her latest piglets, the sow sprawling contentedly on her comfortable bed of straw, with her plump, pink family, vying for the best position to feed from her. She loved to go and count all the piglets and then visit the garden to see the roses. What an array there was. Another tear fell, a tear for time past.

She must collect herself. Today was a big

day for her son and a big day for her. But she didn't feel she was gaining a daughter but only that she was losing her son. Officially. Up to now it was unofficial but now it was for real.

She had tried at first to make friends with the girl, who was to become his fiancée, but it was no use. She was a confident, career woman, independent and modern. There was no common ground. The young couple were going to leave the London flat they shared, buy a house in the nearby town and start their own business. A house with no garden to speak of. The girl had said something about making a garden, but she hadn't listened, she simply hadn't believed her. They would probably just turf it all over. She had no interest in it. They would do what suited them, they didn't need her and she would concentrate on her own garden and her beloved roses and let them get on with it.

She had no duties as 'mother of the bridegroom' beyond trying to look elegant and being gracious, especially to her son's new wife and her family. She knew she looked elegant and as for 'gracious' she would try. She might even invite her new daughter-in-law's mother to tea, while 'the happy couple' were away on their honeymoon. Yes, she would make an effort.

Her wedding limousine arrived and she was whisked away to the village church and ushered to her place to await the service. The wedding ceremony took place but she couldn't follow it. She was concentrating too hard on her composure, determined not to shed a tear. Then the service was over. The organ sang forth, the bride lifted her veil, 'the happy couple' kissed and began to make their way along the aisle, followed by a flurry of little bridesmaids. As they drew level with her, the bride deftly extracted a single, white rose from her exquisite, trailing bridal bouquet.

'For you, to remind you that you promised to help me make a new garden. A garden with lots of roses just like yours, er a rose garden,' she explained with unexpected, faltering earnestness.

They swept on and she clung on to the rose and and thought that maybe the future was going to offer more than she had thought possible and would not be too bad after all. The bride's mother, a plump little woman, smiled at her across the aisle, secure in her daughter's love and delighted with her daughter's gesture.

She left the church as soon as she reasonably could, and walked out into the blinding sunshine of the churchyard. After the photos and before she was transported off to the reception, she stole away in search of Mr Sullivan's grave. She bent down and placed her buttonhole upon it with care, still clutching at the single, white rose.

'It's going to be all right, Mr Sullivan,' she whispered, adding proudly, 'Claire, that's my new daughter-in-law, Claire and I are going to make a garden. Together. Just like yours. A rose garden.'

The Souvenir

There came a lull in the fighting. The heavy German bombardment they had encountered, just outside the village, had forced them to abandon their Bren gun carrier and seek cover in the wayside barn. The enemy firing had ceased for a while. It had ceased deceptively before, only to start up again, when they thought it was safe to continue their advance through occupied France.

The young soldier, of the King's Shropshire Light Infantry, felt in the breast pocket of his uniform for the small wooden box, which he had made in a school woodwork class. Just to feel it safely there was a comfort, because it took him back immediately to that idyllic, summer afternoon in the garden, when the young girl, now his wife, had plucked a rose for him. He had kept it ever since in the box. No thought of war had shadowed the sunny skies that day.

He would write to her soon, if only an army issue postcard with the curt stereotype phrases, which advised the recipient that the sender was alive and well and fighting in a foreign field.

He patted the box and reassured, prepared to continue the grim business of war.

* * *

A sunny day in early June, blessed by a gentle, cooling breeze. The summer of 1937 had been a good year for roses. The garden then was a-bloom with all sorts, ranging from delicate, pale pinks to full-bodied, blowzy roses of deepest crimson. A wonderful, fragrant, carefree summer with nothing to foreshadow what was to befall the world. In the shimmering heat, the young girl seemed to float ethereally in a frock of fine lawn, that hung about her slender frame. The young man had cycled up to meet her from his home at the other end of the village, after lunch with his family. They had planned to go for a Sunday afternoon walk, but first she had to show him the roses. The pink bush was laden with buds ready to burst forth and a few early roses in full flush. She plucked a pink rose, not fully opened and handed it to him.

'For your buttonhole,' she said, smiling shyly.

He thanked her, closed his eyes to

concentrate on inhaling the scent, and fixed the rose in the lapel of his linen jacket. They made a good couple. She was slender and lissom, with brown hair and green eyes. He was fresh-complexioned with dark eyes, tall and athletic. They had met at the village dance, some time ago. She loved to dance and would practice in the house or garden at any opportunity. He took her hand and they strolled through the garden together and out through the meadow beyond. It was a special day, for he was going to propose to her on their return from the walk.

* * *

We were looking through my father's belongings. My mother said she had mis-laid his engraved watch and we had come to the conclusion that it must have been put away with my father's things, when we had got round to this sad task, some weeks after his funeral. I began to trawl through his wardrobe and came across a wooden box about two inches square, old unvarnished wood with a small sickle-hook fastening. I wondered if my father had made it himself. Before I could open it my mother said lightly, 'there's a rose in there,' pointing towards the box.

'What?' I countered, not understanding.

'There's a rose inside that box,' she repeated softly.

I opened it and there indeed was an old and faded rose, carefully preserved since the day she had given it to my father, some seventy years ago. Tawny petals now, brown calyx and grey-green leaves. Not a trace of scent, but tied with a rose-pink cotton thread, it lay on tissue-paper, which had faded to a light brown over the years. My mother crossed the room and stood at my side.

'Yes, you see there it is, the rose I gave your father, all those years ago. Still there.'

Stiff, old fingers stroked the frail petals tenderly. 'Yes, he kept it always. It even went to war with him, all through the war.'

She fell silent. Who knew what memories unspoken were flooding through her mind and heart?

* * *

'I'm going to join up. I have to. You understand darling,' he said simply.

'You must do whatever you feel is right. I just wish, I just wish,' she faltered and he gathered her into his arms and held her close.

'I know, I know darling,' he murmured.

It was the summer of 1939 and they had only been married a few months after a long courtship, while they saved up to get married. She always knew he would join up and do what he thought was right. She felt proud of him, regretful that they had but a short time together as a married couple and fearful for the future.

She saw him off at the station, thinking how dashing he looked. He was bound for Norwich and the barracks and a new life serving King and country. She watched till the train was out of sight. She walked slowly home, not to their dear little house, which was called 'The Haven,' but back to her parents' house. They had decided she would live there, together with her unmarried sister, while both he and her father were away on active service.

In due course the regiment was posted to France and she could only wait and pray. When he returned on leave she could see the change in him immediately. He was leaner, harder, stronger, with an upright, military bearing and a brisk manner. The boy had disappeared forever.

He was now a man, fighting for what he believed in and prepared to lay down his life for the values his country cherished. He was to see more of life in the coming months than in all his untried years to date. There was nothing like the hell of war to turn a boy into a man. It would be his first experience of death. Violent death in the sudden blasting away of comrades, and the lingering agony of the mortally wounded on the field of battle. He would rescue the wounded under fire and see the wretchedness of civilians as they fled with scant possessions, as the war reached out its tentacles to engulf them. He would know both the danger of patrols in enemy held territory and the terror of the front line.

He would assist in the liberation of Concentration Camps and witness their unspeakable legacy. So many facets would contribute to the change of character, the hardening of the boy into the man, and yet through all the 'blood, sweat and tears,' the hardship, terror and sorrow he would treasure the little rose.

The cherished gift from the young woman he was yet to marry had become a sort of talisman, a link to an idyllic, carefree English summer day in peace-time and epitomised that for which he and countless others had been prepared to lay down their lives.

I looked down at the faded flower, a simple rose plucked from a garden during my parents' courtship all those years ago. It betrayed a completely new side to my father, whom I had never thought of as in the least sentimental. My mother of course had known him as a boy, young and carefree, untried by life, and unscathed by war.

I left her to her memories. I needed to walk in the garden among the roses and to let them work their soul-soothing balm, their time-honoured legacy, the alchemy of the rose.

The Prize Winner

The gardening club consisted of a group of twenty or so ladies, of a certain age, who met once a month in the house of a volunteer hostess. The ladies were all keen gardeners and keenly competitive. They were competitive about their gardens, winning the gardening club competitions and the refreshments they offered as hostesses to their gardening club guests.

The gardening club's tried and trusted meeting format was: Welcome with coffee and biscuits, Introduction, Presentation or some instruction, Discussion, Forward Planning, relating to visits to gardens and nurseries, Any Other Business, Tour of the hostess' garden and last but not least Refreshments.

The gardening club had been set up some years ago by three gardening friends, Dilly, Dolly and Dandy.

Dolly was the organiser. She was, as they say, 'a born organiser'. She compulsively organised everything and everybody. She carried sheaves of beautifully, word processed lists for everything and took her role as 'Madame

Chairman' and her chairmanship duties very seriously indeed.

Dandy was the more knowledgeable gardener, if truth were told, and often secretly regretted that she had not pursued a career in horticulture. But she contented herself with reading up on the subject, while promising herself that one day, she would undertake a course in some aspect of the subject, probably design.

Dilly loved gardening and was besotted with roses. It was she, who had introduced the idea of a rose competition. Three competitions actually. A competition for 'the best display of roses in a garden,' 'the best arrangement of cut roses from the garden in a container,' and 'the best individual rose bloom.' There were three separate prizes and the overall best score would merit custody of the silver rose bowl, (funded by the three founding members), for a year, during which time the winner would have her name engraved upon it in perpetuity. The judging panel consisted of two of the three founder members, (which allowed one of them to compete every three years) and two more judges were drawn from the ranks of the club.

This year it was Dilly's turn to compete and

her garden was a sight to behold. Cottage garden style borders, a central old well transformed into a feature and trees at the very end to screen whatever lay beyond. The fences to the sides were clothed in climbers throughout the seasons and the lawn was maintained to perfection. Since the departure of her husband, she had given up the vegetable plot and had converted it to additional lawn and flower beds. The lawn was tended now by her neighbour Henrico, who also looked after the front hedges and any heavy work. He wouldn't think of accepting cash for his labours, so she kept him supplied with wines throughout the year and liqueurs at Christmas.

Henrico was a retired businessman and a keen gardener, whose own garden was immaculate and whose vegetable garden produce, won him prizes at the local gardening association. After his wife died, he also found time to develop a sensory garden for the local Blind Club. His parents were Italian but he had attended an English school, the pronounced Italian accent was an affectation. In his youth, he had found it had quite an influence on the young women he encountered and it had grown up with him and was now an inalienable part of him. To his regret it did not seem to cut any ice with his neighbour Dilly.

The days before the judging, Dilly toiled in the garden prinking and preening and when she retired to bed on the penultimate night before the judging, it was with the delicious languor of a day spent working in the garden and the consequent promise of sound sleep.

She awoke to chaos. Her main rose bed had been vandalised, but on closer examination, she observed that all the rose bushes had been removed with care. The rose garden was however a wasteland. There was no trace of the roses, not a petal, not a bud, not a leaf. All gone. She sank to her knees on the lawn beside the bed and shed bitter tears. Then anger set in. Who could possibly have done this dreadful deed? And why in the run up to the judging? Could it be a jealous club member? Impossible, surely. But the thought reminded her to ring Dolly and then Dandy to explain that she could no longer be considered as an entrant for the competition. Their sympathy and vehemence in condemning the perpetrator made her feel better.

She telephoned Henrico, who said he would be round immediately. He expressed his horror, sympathised and made a constructive suggestion i.e. would container roses be acceptable? If so he could supply the container roses he had been preparing for the charity's sensory garden and these could be inserted into the holes left by the ravaged roses. This would make the rose bed look more furnished and it might even allow her to be part of the competition. Dilly was concerned that Henrico should offer so much of his time and part with his own roses, but he merely said that it was a pleasure to help her and that he wanted her to win the competition anyway.

She began to feel more optimistic, not only about the garden, but life itself. She had a real friend in Henrico, who was worth his weight in gold. When she came to think of it, who else could she turn to in her hour of need, who else would leap to her assistance in this way? Her reverie was in interrupted by Henrico himself, arriving with the first batch of his container roses and announcing that he was about to start work.

She rang Dolly and then Dandy and asked if container roses would be acceptable for the competition 'in the circs'. They replied after due consultation, that 'in the circs' yes they would!'

And so the work continued and by evening the rose bed was restored to its former glory.

Dilly was quite excited about the competition, the judging, and her rescue and couldn't sleep. In the early hours of the morning, she prowled round the house and then made herself a cup of tea. She flicked the curtains and looked out at the peaceful avenue beneath her.

Then she saw a movement – it was Henrico, fiddling about with his trailer, loading black bags. But why at this unearthly hour? As her eyes became accustomed to the darkness, she saw that the bags had rose bushes sticking out of them. And the thought struck her that they were her own rose bushes. And she had a horrible suspicion that she knew now who had ravaged her garden. What on earth was he thinking of? She went back to bed, propped herself up on her pillows and drew the duvet up to her chin in order to think things through.

Henrico had perpetrated the terrible deed and then had presented himself as her rescuer. He had in fact contrived the situation, in order to assume the role of rescuer, a sort of avenging angel, a knight in shining, well in this case, tarnished armour. She suspected he had some feelings for her, but she always kept the relationship on a strictly neighbourly basis. She had gently refused the invitations to supper at his house. 'Nipping it in the bud,' she thought wryly. She didn't want any complications. She didn't want any involvements. She had barely come to terms with her husband going off with his trollop of a secretary. She had no time or inclination for romance in her life. But she was nevertheless grateful that Henrico was going to put everything to rights in time for the competition. And no one would know. She might even win. She was of course angry with Henrico. But she began to realise that he had arranged all this merely to win her over. He must like her rather a lot, and this thought and her rescue, made her feel protected and she quite liked that. She settled herself, wiggled her toes in pleasure and with a mind calmed by rational thought soon fell asleep.

Judging day dawned and her garden was a-bloom. No sign of devastation. All was well. It was a bright, sunny day, the garden was at its best, everyone admired the spectacle and to cap it all she was in due course declared the winner. She had won! This meant that she was the keeper of the silver rose bowl for the year. It was when she was on her way to the jeweller, the next day, to get it engraved that conscience struck. Of course she couldn't claim the prize! Her success was largely due to Henrico's intervention. She ignored the fact that he was the culprit and had caused the devastation in the first place. It was nevertheless through his good offices that she had won. It would have to be his name engraved on the silver bowl. And thus it came to pass. She rang Dolly and then Dandy to explain the situation and suggested that 'in the circs,' Henrico's name should be engraved on the rose bowl. After due consultation they replied that 'in the circs,' 'well, yes!'

She explained all to the judging committee, invited the gardening club en masse to a special, unscheduled, sumptuous summer tea, where she related that her garden had been vandalised by an unknown hand, and then had been restored by her friend and neighbour Henrico. She had felt it only right that his name should be engraved on the rose bowl in these exceptional circumstances. There was a significant pause and then to her relief, everyone applauded in a chorus of approval and Henrico came forward to receive his prize from Dolly and Dandy. He pecked them both on both cheeks.

He then pecked Dilly on both cheeks, squeezed her hand, and waved in acknowledgement to all the ladies of the garden club. Dilly smiled up at him and said, 'thank you Henrico, you saved the day.'

'For you I would do anything,' he affirmed with brio, the accent stronger than ever, still holding her hand. And as she looked at her delighted friends in the garden club, grouped on the velvet lawn, the perfection of the rose garden beyond and Henrico's earnestly beaming face, she could find no reason to doubt him.

The Rose Arbour

They had planned the garden together. This was what Melanie tried to tell herself. Tried to believe. But she knew it was her own mythology. She knew it wasn't true. She had her own ideas and Philip, her husband, had his own ideas about everything, especially the garden. And anyway, when it came down to it, he was going to 'pay the piper,' well the garden designer in this case and she would just have to cut her cloth accordingly. The mixed metaphors jarred but she knew what she meant.

The thing was neither she nor Philip had bargained for his premature death or the onslaught of the illness that preceded it. The situation had got much better between them since the garden issue was resolved. They had worked at the difficulties of the marriage, somehow epitomised by the garden dispute. They had consciously striven to spend more time together and to accommodate the other's point of view. They both felt they had turned a corner. But round that corner came Philip's illness, which turned out to be terminal and meant in his case that he had but a few short months to live.

The garden became the least of their worries. Melanie put aside her feelings about not having the garden she wanted and tried to accept the limitations he imposed. She had, at an earlier stage, undertaken a design course and largely due to this felt, for one thing, that his concept of scale was all wrong. But she accepted his ideas, his plans. Then, as the illness developed, the garden became something they could truly share. She could work on it and Philip could sit and direct her. When his condition permitted, or rather its treatment, in the shape of potentially debilitating chemotherapy, they could visit historic gardens, garden centres and nurseries to get ideas and stock up on plants and for sheer enjoyment and respite. They also had the time to sit and savour the fruits of their labours together, something that they had not had time to do when they were both well, busy working and bringing up the family.

Melanie wanted a rose arbour. She had always wanted a rose arbour. Her grandparents had had a rose arbour, which she had loved as a child. Now, with a chance to design their new garden, she wanted to have a rose arbour of her own. There had never been an opportunity to install such a feature in any of their previous gardens. Philip had always said it was unnecessary and would get in the way. This time again, he was prepared to provide trellises instead and she tried hard to be content with them and concentrated on the planning, the buying and the planting.

Even so she knew the garden would be special and inescapably, a sort of memorial to him. Perhaps that was why he opposed some of her ideas now. Perhaps he didn't want a memorial at all, let alone a rose arbour. There was a dreadful irony in the way that the garden blossomed, the plants thrived and the roses flourished as his health failed, his strength ebbed, and his hold on life weakened, in a sort of strange, ungainly dance with life and death, death and life.

But she never wavered. She knew the roses had to grow and flourish and fulfil their glorious destiny. And in the same way he had to fulfil his destiny, even if it was a very different outcome. Growing the garden on, growing the roses, the creative process helped her to strike a balance with the process of his decline, which she faced every day. Unrelenting, even with brief remissions, it was part of a predestined, downward spiral and she always knew inevitably, irrevocably, inexorably where it would lead.

Meanwhile the summer burgeoned with teeming life. Bees buzzing, heady scents, hot days, and the garden in different mood in the evening with the white plants singing out against the dusk perhaps in defiance. Her pink and white climbing roses defined the trellises and they would sit in the garden, when he was strong enough, and drink in the scents and the sights. They would sip a glass of wine and the irony of dusks of wine and roses struck her with some force. It would be his last summer.

There was something so poignant about the roses having long lives ahead of them, while his life was ebbing away at a ridiculously early age, just 50. He wouldn't see the kids, a boy and a girl, through University or give his daughter's hand in marriage. Philip had asked her father for his permission to marry her and in his endearingly old-fashioned way assumed that his daughter's prospective fiancé would do the same. He wouldn't be a grandfather and he wouldn't continue his work and attain the ultimate industry recognition and accolades that were his due. There would be no more time to sort out their marriage. They had run out of health and strength and time.

And all summer long the roses bloomed, flourished and prospered. When the summer peaked and the year began to turn, some of the earlier flowering roses had already gone over. It was a time of waiting for the second flush and the later clematis. He had nothing to wait for, nothing to anticipate, only the gradual, painful passing of his life and the slow miasma of decline into pain-relieved oblivion.

On his death Melanie had the loss, the grief and the formalities of death to cope with and the almost unbearable pain of the children's grief to suffer. She had to be strong for the children, even though they were growing up and away at university. Immediately after Philip's initial diagnosis, they had sorted out the practicalities together, the finances, the business side of things. The plan was for her to stay put for a least six months after his death and then downsize. Then she would look for a smaller house and garden and take advantage of this to move nearer her parents, anticipating their need of her as the years took their toll. The truth was that she felt she needed to mark the end of the 25 years of their marriage. She needed to draw a line, if that were possible. A new chapter.

The time came to start to look for the new house. After some weeks of fruitless searching, the Estate Agent suggested that she looked at an old cottage, which he felt would be of interest. Melanie reminded him that she was not looking for 'an old cottage.' He countered by saying that she had made it clear to him that the garden would be important to her. And this garden, although in need of a lot of work, a challenge in fact, had been spectacular in its day, and he felt she should have a look at it. She listened and began to consider that she needed precisely that sort of challenge. She didn't need a new house, what she really needed was a new garden. The challenge of a garden to reclaim and to develop to her own design.

The property was tucked away at the end of the village. It had been the gardener's cottage, part of an old estate many years ago and then had been sold off with all the other estate dwellings. The front garden was bordered by a rickety, wooden fence, which had seen better days. The board, not quite nailed to the gate, announced 'The Old Rose Garden.' The front garden was small and she could see at a glance that the cottage itself was quaint, quirky and charming and deceptively larger than it seemed, although screened by a raft of untidy hollyhocks, ranging from pale pink to deepest red and yellow and white. But she most of all wanted to see the garden. The Estate Agent said he had lots of calls to catch up with on his mobile and she could take her time to explore before they had a look inside the cottage.

Melanie walked slowly through the rampant, overgrown, neglected back garden, which revealed only the faintest traces of what it had been. Generous curved borders, and the remains of a lawn. There was a vegetable plot beyond, flanked by apple trees, and rows of fruit bushes. To their side she came upon an old rose arbour. It was secluded, set at an angle and neglected, but nevertheless a sound and sturdy enough, seasoned, wooden structure. She sat on the seat and looked at the raggle-taggle of old roses climbing up and through it. She envisaged the original owner picking his fruit and setting his basket on the seat beside him to hull and prepare his harvest of red currants, black currants, and raspberries.

Melanie knew with mounting, unfamiliar

certainty that this neglected garden, if painfully won, was somehow meant to be hers. She had finally caught up with her destiny in the shape of a garden to develop and grow on just for herself, her memories and her roses. And inescapably, it was as if her very own rose arbour had claimed her at last.

Evenlode

'The sea was in his blood.' That's what they said. 'The sea was in his blood.' As if that made it acceptable and tidy and all right, when he drowned at sea. But his wife didn't feel it was all right. Not at all.

James had taken his beloved boat out on a cross-channel sailing trip. Bill Woodstock, from the local sailing club had intended to go with him, but had cried off unexpectedly at the last minute and so James had set off without him, as he had several times before. He would stay with friends in France as usual for a couple of days before making the return trip. This time he welcomed the unexpected opportunity to have some time to think things through without Bill's boisterous presence. But he knew deep down that he would have to settle for the status quo as far as his marriage was concerned. It was too late to undertake any upheaval. There was no question now of separation let alone divorce. But retirement was looming and he had no relish for the concept. And he knew that the time was coming when he should probably talk to his wife about it and discuss their future and for that matter his past. He had come to believe that he owed her that at least.

But on this trip something unforeseen had happened. 'An accident,' they said. Certainly, the weather had very suddenly, unexpectedly worsened. James had tried unsuccessfully to rescue another crew member, a young girl, who had been swept overboard and had drowned. James had then been trapped under the boat by his safety harness and had suffered the same fate. A nearby vessel had recovered the girl's body and reported the drifting, unmanned sailing boat to the English Coastguard. They had despatched the Fishery Protection Patrol vessel, which was in the vicinity. Having retrieved the man's body from under the boat and secured custody of the young girl's body, they had taken the sailing boat in tow to the local port.

She had had to undertake the grisly identification of James's remains and had been supported in this by Bill Woodstock, who had been such a stalwart and who had stood by her throughout all the admin, proceedure and formalities. James's boat had survived without a scratch and had eventually been returned to her, or at least to the sailing club. 'Evenlode,' such a beautiful craft, so graceful and so special to him, the love of her husband's life, her deadly rival and now as she saw it his killer.

She had no interest in the sea, she couldn't sail or even swim. But despite this most significant of all the unshared elements in their lives, they had somehow got together and stayed together. He had called her in the early days at least 'his little landlubber.' And she always understood that sailing was his passion and that his sailing boat would therefore feature hugely in his affection and his life. She had no choice but to accept it.

While she occupied her time with her garden and her roses in her childless, lonely marriage, she would often reflect that 'Evenlode's hold on her husband was not unlike that of a mistress. She knew nothing about sailing or the sea but she had often wondered if it was entirely safe for James to sail single-handed across the Channel, whenever Bill couldn't go with him.

But it transpired that James had rarely actually sailed solo, having often been accompanied by his daughter, who was a highly competent sailor. James had apparently seen to that. It was only when two bodies had been recovered and Bill had identified the young girl's body that she had been made aware that James had had a daughter. Bill explained gently that the three of them used to sail together. It was all a huge shock for her and she began to feel that the man she mourned, her husband of many years was more like a stranger to her, and that the marriage had been a sham.

Afterwards the condolences were many, from James's former colleagues at the practice, from his friends at the the golf club, the sailing club, and the sailing charity for the disabled, with which James was so involved and which was operated from the sailing club. The funeral was private, just for the remnants of the family and Bill Woodstock.

The memorial service, held sometime later at Bill's suggestion, was quite a big affair. It was as if she hadn't quite grasped the full extent of her husband's involvement with the life of the local community, which she had chosen not to share.

Later in the reading of the will, she had to hide the fact that she had not been aware that

James had a seventeen year old daughter, for which he had made due provision and that he had willed his boat to the Trust for his sailing charity. Perhaps he had just taken it for granted that she would realise what 'Evenlode's destiny would be. That, at least, must have been an oversight. She chose not to believe that he hadn't cared whether she knew or not. However, she couldn't of course ignore the fact that he had failed to tell her that he had a daughter.

In due course it was the sailing club, who proposed that they should honour James's memory in the breeding of a rose to be named after him. The rose would have pride of place in the clubhouse garden, which was well maintained by several non-sailing spouses. A proportion of the sale of the rose through the breeder's catalogue would benefit the sailing charity.

The proposal was, in truth, meant to be a distraction and a consolation for her, as her love of roses was well-known. The committee involved her in the process of approaching the local, nationally acclaimed rose breeder and of coming up with a name to acknowledge the new rose's parentage. The rose was to be dramatic with the colours of sunset and a strong fragrance and various names were suggested by a battery of interested parties.

She longed to be free of it all, her betrayal, her anger, and her grief. She also longed to be free of all the red tape, 'Evenlode' herself, the condolences, and the pursuit of the rose. With the discovery of James's daughter and her tragic loss, she yearned even more for solitude, the solace of her home and garden, and especially her roses. But there was still one more task to perform, for she had finally and formally to announce the name of the rose to the club.

But when it came to it, she found that she had always known there could only be one name for James's rose. And it was as if she had at last made peace with her beautiful, implacable, deadly rival. The rival who had cost her her husband's life and had thereby given her an unprecedented insight into his other, parallel life. She said simply, with a new-found, cathartic serenity, 'James loved that boat so much, we must name the rose after her. We'll name his rose, 'Evenlode.'

The Last of the Roses

There came the expected knocking at the door. She opened it to welcome her mother, whose lovely face was bright as a child's, her blue eyes shining.

'Merry Christmas!' her mother greeted her, clutching brightly wrapped Christmas presents and holding out a carefully tied bunch of rosebuds, 'here you are darling, the last of the roses.'

The faded richness of the colours were reminiscent of an old tapestry, recalling the beauty of what they had been in their prime and still exuding the most delicate of scents. It had been the same nearly every Christmas for the last twenty odd years. On Christmas morning the bells would ring out their joyful summons from St Saviour's, whose churchyard bordered the garden of her block of flats. Soon afterwards her parents would enter the communal front door and make their way up the stairs to her own front door. It was part of the tradition of their Christmas. Most Sundays she went to their home for lunch but on special anniversaries throughout the year and especially at Christmas, she invited her parents to lunch with her.

The modern purpose-built block, divided into three sections of four flats, overlooked the little Victorian church, set in a grassed churchyard, bordered by large, mature trees and studded with but a few graves. The bells summoned the faithful every Sunday and at other times rang out to celebrate weddings, or to toll their doleful homage for funerals. The arrival of the Christmas tree at the church in time for Advent Sunday always proclaimed the start of the festive season. A dark, familiar shape it took up the whole of one of the stained glass windows, opposite her bedroom window, and when lit up was a magnificent, bejewelled sight, casting a multicoloured, dancing reflection on the snow or grass beneath. On Christmas Eve she would make a point of leaving the bedroom window and the curtains open, so that she could enjoy the Christmas tree and hear the gentle strains of carols floating up on the frosty air.

Now that both her parents had died, this would be her first Christmas alone. The remaining family were too old to travel, or to have guests. She had, however, received invitations from friends, all of which she had declined, as she felt she had to get to grips with the new order. More than that she wanted time on her own to indulge and to savour all the memories of Christmas past. She hadn't of course bothered with any Christmas decorations. She didn't feel like it after her mother's death earlier in the year and it would be inappropriate, but it was mainly because she couldn't bear to rifle through the box of Christmas decorations added to over the years. She had however, bought as always a miniature potted fir tree to stand on the corner table and had added just a string or two of delicate tinsel and a small silver star for the top.

This year she had inherited her mother's own box of Christmas decorations, which included a small, exquisitely made Father Christmas figure from more than 60 years ago, before her marriage. She remembered him from her childhood and that he always had pride of place on the mantelpiece. Clad in a red-hooded, fur-trimmed fabric robe down to his long, black suede boots, he sported a painted, cheery face above a long white beard, and whiskers. He was bedecked with miniature wooden toys ready to deliver, a spotted dog, a brightly-painted drum, and a spinning top. There was also a small, silver tree with swathes of white, silk fringing with glittering, silver filigree threads running through it to look like frost. She had found that she wasn't up to dealing with any of her mother's belongings for the time being and her mother's Christmas decorations remained in their box.

Every Christmas she would gather sprigs from the shrubs in the garden, she had made, when she had first come to live in the flat, to arrange in a vase and to make a wreath for the front door. The greenery and vigour of the traditional holly, ivy, mistletoe, were most welcome and life affirming at this so-called dormant time of year. Her garden also boasted jasmine, winter honeysuckle, the early viburnum, red-stemmed cornus, witch hazel and her favourite wintersweet.

And of course there would be the rose-buds from her parents' garden. Her father would spare the best of the last buds, cut them on Christmas Eve and keep them somewhere cool. Her mother would painstakingly tie each bud with a matching thread, to keep them from opening too soon.

She sat on the sofa, staring out over

the churchyard, carpeted in snow, the trees magically transformed into its strange, ethereal, mysterious guardians, the gravestones half-masked with snow. She stared out for sometime, with no regard for time passing. Then the bells rang out, a special peal for Christmas morning to startle and shatter the silence, which stalked her. She listened until they had fallen silent and then on an impulse sprang up to open her front door. There was nobody else in the four flats, nobody in the other three blocks. Everyone was always away for Christmas Day, and most people for longer.

She stared into the deep stairwell of cold, echoing emptiness. The chill, eerie silence enveloped, engulfed and overwhelmed her. She shivered, felt faint and leant against the door frame for support. Then gradually she became aware of a trace of something in the air, elusive, indefinable, but at once strangely familiar. She struggled to identify it, then recognition flooded through her as the fragrance wafted towards her and into the flat. With a leap of her heart she knew what it was for certain. The faint but unmistakable fragrance of her mother's traditional Christmas offering, 'the last of the roses.'